PIRATE SCHOOL
The Curse of Snake Island

by Brian James
illustrated by Jennifer Zivoin

Grosset & Dunlap

For all my friends from Fleetwood!—BJ

To Mom & Dad, Katie, Steven, and my
husband Romeo—for all your
encouragement and support.— JZ

GROSSET & DUNLAP
Published by the Penguin Group
Penguin Group (USA) Inc., 375 Hudson Street, New York, New York 10014, U.S.A.
Penguin Group (Canada), 90 Eglinton Avenue East, Suite 700, Toronto,
Ontario, Canada M4P 2Y3
(a division of Pearson Penguin Canada Inc.)
Penguin Books Ltd, 80 Strand, London WC2R 0RL, England
Penguin Ireland, 25 St Stephen's Green, Dublin 2, Ireland
(a division of Penguin Books Ltd)
Penguin Group (Australia), 250 Camberwell Road, Camberwell, Victoria 3124, Australia
(a division of Pearson Australia Group Pty Ltd)
Penguin Books India Pvt Ltd, 11 Community Centre, Panchsheel Park,
New Delhi - 110 017, India
Penguin Group (NZ), Cnr Airborne and Rosedale Roads, Albany,
Auckland 1310, New Zealand
(a division of Pearson New Zealand Ltd)
Penguin Books (South Africa) (Pty) Ltd, 24 Sturdee Avenue, Rosebank,
Johannesburg 2196, South Africa

Penguin Books Ltd, Registered Offices:
80 Strand, London WC2R 0RL, England

Library of Congress Control Number: 2006033100

ISBN 978-0-448-44574-8   10 9 8 7 6 5 4 3 2 1

Chapter 1
Slippery Stink

I covered my nose as I looked into the tank on the main deck of our ship, the *Sea Rat*. It was filled with stinky fish guts.

Inna took a peek, too, then covered her eyes. She was the only pirate kid in the whole world who was afraid of everything gross and dirty. You could tell that from looking at her, too. She always wore fancy dresses and stuff.

"Sink me! We're not really going to walk across that, are we, Pete?" Vicky asked me in surprise.

I looked at the skinny plank that lay across the fish tank. It was only the tiniest bit wider than my feet. One slip meant smelling like rotten fish for a month!

"Aye! We have to," I said. "Rotten Tooth is never going to teach us any real pirate stuff. Not unless we prove that we're brave enough."

Rotten Tooth was supposed to be our teacher here at Pirate School. But so far, we hadn't learned a thing!

"Pete's right!" Aaron said, his dark eyes flashing. As Vicky's twin brother, he never missed a chance to disagree with her. Vicky and Aaron look just alike. Except Aaron's brown hair is shorter than Vicky's. "We've been here at Pirate School for two whole months, and all Rotten Tooth has taught us is how to swab the deck!"

Rotten Tooth is the first mate on our ship. Captain Stinky Beard made him our teacher on the first day of Pirate School. He said the best pirate would make the best teacher.

Rotten Tooth didn't like that one bit. He didn't like the whole idea of Pirate School. It was the captain's idea to invite us here and start the school. "Training mangy kids is a waste of me time," Rotten Tooth told us when the captain wasn't around. "Ye ain't fit for pirating, so I'll be teaching you cleaning instead."

We wanted to tell the captain. But we knew if we did, Rotten Tooth would turn us into shark bait in the blink of an eye. So none of us were any closer to being real pirates than we were the day we got there. And Pirate School was the only reason we left our old ships to join up on the *Sea Rat*.

"Did our captains send us here to be deckhands or pirates?" I asked my friends.

"Aye, pirates! But how is crossing that stink pit going to change Rotten Tooth's mind?" Vicky asked.

"Yeah, how?" Gary wondered. Gary was the youngest kid at Pirate School. Even though he was only nine, his parents thought he was ready to become a pirate. So they sent him to live on the *Sea Rat*— just like the rest of our parents did.

"Because it's an old pirate test," I

replied. I'd lived on a pirate ship my whole life. All ten years. Well, nine and three-quarters, to be exact. That's longer than anyone else. So I knew lots of pirate stuff that they didn't.

"If someone wanted to become a pirate, first they had to walk across this plank," I explained.

"Aye?" Inna asked, peeking back into the tank and making a face.

"Aye!" I said. "It proves you can keep your balance. Plus, anyone brave enough to risk smelling like that stuff is brave enough to face any danger on the sea!" I pointed to the fish guts down below.

"I guess it's worth a try," Vicky finally agreed.

"Aye!" I said. "We'll show Rotten Tooth that we're ready for pirating."

I stared at the slimy plank. It looked very slippery.

"Stop being such a scallywag and go already!" Aaron shouted. *Scallywag* was pirate speak for calling me a scaredy-cat.

But I was no scallywag!

I was a pirate. One day, I might even be the captain of my very own ship. Captain Pete the pirate.

Just then, a wave shook the *Sea Rat*.

Inna gulped.

"Maybe we should wait until the sea is steady," I said.

"Gangway, scallywags! I'll go first," Aaron said.

"You're going to get a face full of fish stink!" Vicky warned.

"Arrr! I can do it easy," Aaron told her. "In fact, I could do it blindfolded," he added.

"Could not!" Vicky shouted.

"Could too!" Aaron shouted back.

"Prove it, then!" Vicky said.

"Fine! I will!" he said.

I shook my head. Aaron was always showing off.

Aaron marched over to the tank and climbed up the side.

"Inna, can I borrow your bandana to use as a blindfold?" he asked.

"No way!" Inna shouted. Then she covered it with both hands. "I'm not letting you get fish guts on my pretty bandana."

"I won't. I promise," Aaron begged.

"You absolutely promise?" she asked.

Vicky grabbed the blindfold out of Inna's hands before Aaron had a chance to answer. "Enough stalling!" Vicky said, handing the bandana to her brother.

Aaron tied the blindfold over his eyes.

"This looks like a bad idea," Gary said.

"Blimey! You think everything's a bad idea!" Vicky snapped.

"Not everything," he said. "Just the ideas that can get us into trouble."

"We won't get in trouble, because I'm not going to fall!" Aaron shouted as he got ready to take his first step.

"Be careful!" I warned. "The first step is the slipperiest!"

Sure enough, Aaron slipped as soon as he stepped on the board. Inna covered her eyes. She didn't want to see her bandana get ruined.

But Aaron waved his arms around and caught his balance. "See . . ."

Just then a big hand came down on Aaron's shoulder.

"Uh-oh," I mumbled.

It was Rotten Tooth!

Rotten Tooth was the meanest, ugliest-looking pirate on the ship! His hair was green and looked like seaweed. His beard was parted in the middle and pointed out like two furry tusks. And then there were his teeth! They were just as green as his hair and sharper than a shark's.

"ARRRRR!" Rotten Tooth growled.

Aaron was so startled that he lost his balance. His feet slipped out from under him and he slid right into Rotten Tooth.

CRASH!

They fell into the tank in one stinky second!

"We're in really big serious trouble now," Gary said.

When Rotten Tooth poked his head up, I thought I could see steam coming out of his ears.

He lifted Aaron up in the air and put him on the deck. Aaron was dripping with gross, yucky gook.

We all held our noses. Then Rotten Tooth climbed out. He smelled even more rotten than usual.

"We're sorry," I mumbled. "It was a test to show you that we're ready to be pirates."

"AYE! AND YOU ALL FAILED!" Rotten Tooth shouted.

"We didn't mean to cause any trouble," Inna whispered.

"QUIET!" Rotten Tooth roared. "One more word and I toss you all overboard! I've heard enough from you pollywogs today."

He wiped the muck off his face. Then he told us to follow him. "Arrr! I'm putting you somewhere where the punishment will fit the crime."

As he led us below deck, we ran into Captain Stinky Beard.

"Ahoy! Taking the little shipmates below deck for a lesson?" he asked Rotten Tooth.

"Aye! I'm going to teach them a lesson all right," he said.

I had a terrible sinking feeling in my stomach—and it wasn't just because of the stink coming from Aaron as he walked in front of me.

Chapter 2
Here a Mess, There a Mess

"Scrub! Scrub! Scrub!" Aaron mumbled as he knelt on the kitchen floor. "This *stinks*!"

"I think it's you that stinks," Vicky said, holding her nose with one hand and scrubbing the floor with her other hand.

Aaron made a face at her. Then he sniffed. He really did stink!

"I could've made it," he said. "If Rotten Tooth hadn't shown up and startled me, I mean."

Inna poked her head out from behind the stack of messy dishes that she was washing. She gave Aaron a dirty look. She still hadn't forgiven him about her bandana, or for getting us put on the filthiest job on the ship . . . kitchen duty.

"Look at the mess you got us in," Vicky said to her brother. "We'll be washing dishes for the rest of the day!"

"Arrr, don't blame me!" Aaron shouted. "It was Pete's silly test that got us into this mess."

I put my head down. "I was just trying to prove to Rotten Tooth that we were ready to learn real pirate stuff," I said. "Boy, did that backfire."

"Aye, you can say that again!" Aaron sneered with a face full of soap bubbles. "This is going to take forever to clean up."

Vicky held her nose again and looked at Aaron. "*You're* going to take forever to clean up!"

I looked around. Aaron was right.

The kitchen and dining area were a disaster. There were piles of dirty dishes stacked up everywhere. Some of the piles were taller than me! Plus, there was slop spilled all over the floor and against the walls. Pirates aren't known for their table manners.

"I really sunk our ship, huh?" I asked my friends. "Rotten Tooth will never teach us now. We'd be better off back on our old ships."

"Not true, matey!" Gary said. "On my old ship, I'd be cleaning this kitchen all by myself."

"Aye!" Vicky said. "On our last ship, Aaron caused so much trouble, the captain was ready to make fish food of us. The day before we shipped out, Aaron ripped the sail right in half!"

"Aye?" I asked.

"Aye!" Aaron answered with a little smile.

Inna looked up from the grimy food gunk in the sink and nodded her head. "And besides, Pete, you were only trying to help," she said. "I guess Rotten Breath never heard of that test. I'm sure you'll come up with another plan. A better plan."

"Really? You think so?" I asked.

"*Aye!*" all of my friends answered.

I felt a little better already. I knew I

could think of something. After all, we were the brightest pirate kids on the sea. Captain Stinky Beard said so himself the day we got here.

"There's got to be a way to show Rotten Tooth that we would make tip-top pirates," I said.

"But how?" Vicky asked.

Suddenly, Gary raised his hand up in the air.

"I know!" he shouted. "We could hypnotize Rotten Tooth."

I scratched my head and thought about it. "But how do you hypnotize someone?" I asked.

"Easy!" Gary said. Then he turned to Inna. "Can I borrow your necklace?"

Inna's necklace was silvery and shiny. I could even see my reflection in it.

"Nobody's borrowing anything of mine ever again!" She

covered up her necklace with both of her hands.

"Fine," Gary said. "I'll just pretend, then." He mimicked holding the shiny necklace in front of his eyes and let it sway back and forth.

"That doesn't do anything," Aaron said doubtfully.

"Does too," Gary said. "On the last ship I was on, they had a book of old pirate

tales. One of them was about a captain that got hypnotized."

"Hogwash," Aaron said.

"Arrr, if it's in a book, it's got to be true!" Vicky said.

"Aye!" Gary agreed. "And after he got hypnotized, the captain's eyes went all crossed and he stumbled around like this." As Gary showed us, he stumbled right into a stack of dishes! Luckily I was there to catch the dishes before they fell.

"Maybe we need a different plan," I said.

"We could lock him in a room with Aaron until the stink drives him crazy!" Vicky said. We all laughed.

Aaron picked up a mop and held it like a sword. "If there was only some way we could get ol' Rotten Face to bring us ashore when we got to Snake Island," he said. "Then he'd see what we could do!"

Aaron began jumping around the room. He swung the mop, pretending to fight off the giant snake that was rumored to live on Snake Island.

Legend had it that the giant snake was guarding a treasure. And Captain Stinky Beard just happened to have a map that led to the snake's secret cave.

"I would do anything to be able to help find that treasure!" Aaron said.

Find the treasure?

"AVAST! THAT'S IT!" I shouted and threw my arms up in the air. I would've danced around, too, except it's not very piratey.

"What's it?" Aaron asked.

"*We* find the treasure first, that's it!" I said. "If we find it before the rest of the crew, then it would prove that we're good pirates. It won't be easy, but it could work. As long as we work as a team," I told them. "So, is everyone onboard?"

Aaron put the mop to his side and saluted. "Aye aye!"

"Aye! That's good thinking, Pete!" Vicky said.

"Aye, but will it be dangerous?" Gary asked.

I shrugged. "We won't know until we try. Besides, pirates are supposed to be brave," I reminded Gary.

"Well, I guess I'm in," he said.

We all turned to Inna.

"Can I cover my eyes if we see any snakes?" Inna asked. Then she made a face like she was seasick. "Snakes are even ickier than fish guts."

"You can cover your eyes if you want to," I told her. And finally she agreed to come along.

I smiled real wide.

Everything was coming together.

"One question?" Vicky asked. "How are we ever going to pull this off?"

"Leave that to me," I said. "I'll come up with something." And as we all went back to our chores, I tried to think up a plan.

Chapter 3
Top-Sneaky Mission

The next morning, we were all up early.

We raced up to the main deck to report for school.

"Maybe Rotten Head won't be mad anymore," Aaron said.

But as soon as I saw Rotten Tooth's face, I knew we were still on his bad side. There was one good thing. Captain Stinky Beard was with him. Rotten Tooth never yelled at us too much when the captain was around.

"Fall in!" he roared, and we all formed a straight line.

He paced back and forth. I had to hold my breath every time he passed. He still hadn't taken a bath. In fact, I don't think he'd ever taken a bath!

"Listen up, ye sea dogs!" he growled. "I got a mighty smart lesson for you today."

I started to smile. Maybe we were finally going to learn something.

"Are we going to swashbuckle?" Aaron asked excitedly.

"Aye!" Rotten Tooth said, and we all cheered.

"Such fine little buckoes!" Captain Stinky Beard said. "Always wanting to learn." Then he wished us luck and went off.

"I can't believe it," I said. "We're really going to learn how to swashbuckle!"

"Aye," Rotten Tooth said again. Then he reached behind him and grabbed five mops. "And here be ye swords!"

Our hearts sank. We weren't going to be learning anything after all.

"I want this deck spotless," Rotten Tooth said. "I don't want to be seeing a speck of dirt, ye savvy?"

"Maybe he should get off of it, then," Aaron whispered in my ear. But Rotten Tooth had better hearing than a whale.

He turned to Aaron and showed his famously green teeth. "One more peep out of you," he warned, "and it's back in the fish tank!"

Aaron quickly closed his mouth.

"Aye, that's I was thought," Rotten Tooth said. "Now get to work, ye barnacles!" he snapped as he walked away.

Vicky groaned. "Pirate School? This is more like Chore School."

"Aye," everyone agreed.

24

I didn't complain, though. Cleaning the deck was the best chore Rotten Tooth could have given us in order for my plan to work.

"Ahoy, guys, listen up!" I gathered my friends into a huddle. "I came up with a plan last night."

"I hope this one doesn't stink," Aaron said.

I shot Aaron a look. "No, this is a good plan. Captain Stinky Beard keeps all the treasure maps in his quarters, right?"

"Right," Vicky said.

"And his quarters are in the main cabin, which is over there," I said, pointing to the cabin door behind us.

"So?" Aaron said.

"So, we sneak in and make a copy of the map," I told them.

"Aye! Good thinking," Gary said.

"Aaron and Vicky, you stay outside and keep watch. If Rotten Tooth comes back, distract him."

"Aye! I'll take care of Ol' Rotten Head,"

25

Aaron said, pretending his mop was a sword.

"Gary, you'll wait outside Captain Stinky Beard's room in case anyone gets past Aaron and Vicky," I said.

"Aye aye, Pete!"

"Inna, you'll come inside with me," I said. "You have the neatest handwriting, and the map might have a lot of words to copy."

Then we all put our hands together in the circle and gave a pirate cheer:

"SWASHBUCKLING, SAILING, FINDING TREASURE, TOO!

"BECOMING PIRATES IS WHAT WE WANT TO DO!"

After we finished our cheer, Vicky and Aaron started mopping the deck. They kept their eyes open for anyone heading toward us. Then they gave us the thumbs-up. So Gary, Inna, and I snuck into the main cabin.

The main cabin of the *Sea Rat* was filled with all kinds of cool things like telescopes, model ships, ocean maps, and, of course, treasure! We wanted to stop and look through everything, but we were on a mission.

"If anyone comes, give us a shout," I told Gary as I pushed open the creaky door to Captain Stinky Beard's room.

"Aye!"

As soon as the door shut behind us, I heard Gary shout. I rushed back out, but no one was there.

"Just practicing," Gary said.

I shook my head and went back in.

Inside, the room was a mess. I would never be allowed to keep my room that messy!

I looked at all the piles on top of Captain Stinky Beard's desk. There must have been a hundred maps. "It's going to be impossible to find the map we need."

"No it won't," Inna said.

"Sure it will," I said.

"No it won't. Look, I've found it!" And Inna was already copying the map of Snake Island onto a blank piece of paper.

"How did you find it so quickly?" I asked.

"Easy," she said. "Since that's where we're going right now, I just looked on the top of the pile."

I had to admit, Inna was one clever pirate! Maybe a little too clean, but clever!

Just as Inna finished copying the map, we heard Gary shout. Then we heard a thundering *CRASH*!

I cracked open the door. There was Gary. And Captain Stinky Beard! They were under a pile of junk! I slapped my forehead.

We were doomed.

"What are you kids doing in here?" the captain asked once he was back on his feet.

One wrong answer and he'd be as mad as Rotten Tooth!

Inna stepped up in front of him.

"Sir, we just came here to ask you if we could have a sleepover on the beach," she said politely. It was brilliant! It was the perfect cover. It was also the second part of my plan. *And* it was going to get us out of trouble.

"You mean at Snake Island?" Captain Stinky Beard asked.

We all nodded.

He scratched his beard. "I don't see the harm in it," he said. We all clapped our hands and thanked him. "But aren't you afraid of snakes?" he asked Inna.

Even the *thought* of snakes made Inna feel sick. But she put on her bravest face. "Not at all," she lied.

Captain Stinky Beard smiled. "I guess Rotten Tooth's teaching is paying off. You'll be fine pirates before you know it."

If he only knew!

Chapter 4
Puzzling Puzzle

After our chores were done, Rotten Tooth told us to scram. "I don't want to be seeing your faces until the sun comes up tomorrow. And even then will be too soon," he said.

That was fine with us. We didn't want to smell him anymore, either!

"Let's climb up to the crow's nest," I suggested.

The crow's nest is our secret spot on the ship. That's because we're the only ones that love to climb up there. Don't tell anyone, but most pirates don't really like to climb. They're afraid of heights. They only do it because it's part of the job. But *shhhh*! That's a pirate secret!

"Let's look at the map," Vicky said once we were at the top.

"Aye, let's! I see why they call it Snake Island," I said, unrolling the map. The whole island was all twisty and shaped like a snake.

Besides copying the picture of the island, Inna had copied down lots of words.

"What's that say?" Vicky asked. She pointed to some words written on the top of the map.

" 'To break the snake's curse, use the curse in reverse,' " Inna read.

"What does that mean?" Aaron asked.

"Maybe it means you need to walk backward when you see the giant snake," Gary suggested.

"Don't be silly," Vicky said. "It means you have to go back in time to *before* you got cursed."

"That's sillier than walking backward," Aaron said with a laugh.

"Is not!" Vicky shouted.

"Is too!"

I waved my arms in the air for them to stop. "Guys, we don't even know what the curse is," I said. "We have to find that out before we know how to break it."

Aaron and Vicky both folded their arms and turned their backs to each other. That's what they always did when they were trying really hard to stop arguing.

Inna put her finger up to her mouth. That meant she was thinking. Then she pointed her finger up in the air real fast.

That meant she had thought of something good.

"Clegg could help us!" she shouted.

Clegg was the oldest pirate on the *Sea Rat*. He knew *everything*! Plus, he didn't mind us asking him questions.

"Aye! I bet he knows all about Snake Island," I said.

"Arrr!" everyone agreed. If anyone could tell us about the curse, it was Clegg.

So we grabbed onto the ropes hanging from the crow's nest and swung down to the deck. We all landed on our feet. Well, everyone except Gary. He always landed on his butt. He said it was a softer landing that way.

Clegg was easy to find. He was the only pirate with a gray beard and an eye patch. And he was always in the same place, fishing off the back of the boat.

He turned his one good eye toward us as we ran up to him. "Ahoy there, little shipmates!" he called out with a smile.

"Ahoy, right back!" I said.

"Come here for a story, have ye?" Clegg asked.

I shook my head.

"Not today," I told him. Then, in my most serious voice, I told Clegg that we had some very, very, very important things to ask him.

"Aye?" he asked.

"Aye!" we all answered.

I looked all around to make sure no one was spying. Then I leaned in close and whispered in Clegg's ear. "We need to know everything you know about the curse of Snake Island."

Clegg took a good look at us.

"Do ye think you're old enough for a scary story like that?" Clegg asked.

I stood up as straight and tall as I could. So did all of my friends. "Aye," I said.

Then Clegg nodded his head and began to tell us the secrets of that spooky place.

Chapter 5
Snake Eyes

"YUCK! YUCK! AND TRIPLE YUCK!" Inna shouted once we were back in the crow's nest. "There's no way I'm going on that island!"

Clegg had told us all about the giant snake. He said the snake put a curse on anyone trying to get at the treasure. "Any bucko who looks into the snake's eyes will turn into a snake," he'd said.

Inna did not like the story one bit. "The only thing worse than *seeing* a snake is *being* a snake!"

"Quit sniveling! Ol' Clegg was just yanking our timbers with that spooky story," Aaron told her.

"How do you know?" Vicky asked.

Aaron closed his eyes and lifted his chin up. It was what Vicky called his know-it-all face. "Because," he said, "curses aren't real."

"You don't know that for sure," she challenged him.

"Sure I do," Aaron said. "Everybody knows that. Right, Pete?"

I shook my head.

I wasn't so sure. Clegg had never fibbed to us before.

"Well, I'm no scallywag! Curse or no curse, I'm going after that treasure," Aaron said.

For once Vicky agreed with Aaron. "Arrr! Me too!" she said. "We came to Pirate School to be pirates, not scallywags."

I thought about all the things we'd learned. So far, Rotten Tooth had taught us how to clean, scrub, and mop. I wanted to learn how to swashbuckle, sail, and find buried treasure. This was our only chance.

"Aye," I said. "I'm going, too."

I wasn't about to let one giant snake stop me. At least, I hoped there was only one. Two giant snakes would've stopped me.

I double-checked the map.

Yep!

Only one giant snake was drawn on there.

That was a relief.

I was just about to ask Gary if he was still coming along when he started shouting. "Land ho! Land ho!" he called out. He was pointing straight ahead at a little island. The island was twisty and

curvy. It was Snake Island, dead ahead.

"Land ho! Let's go, buckoes!" Aaron shouted.

I looked at Gary. Gary shrugged. "It's only one snake, right?" he asked.

"Only one. I double-checked."

Next, I looked at Inna. But she shook her head. She didn't want to come.

"Please," I begged. "You're the best at reading maps. Without you, we'll get lost for sure."

Inna shook her head. "No way! I don't want to get turned into a snake."

I reminded her about our deal. "You can cover your eyes anytime we see a snake. If your eyes are covered, then the giant snake can't put a curse on you."

"I guess that's true," Inna said. Then she finally agreed to come along. "But if I get turned into a snake, I'm biting you first!"

Chapter 6
Heads Up

Rotten Tooth stood on the beach as we came ashore. He took one step and blocked our way. His voice roared like thunder. "And just where do you pollywogs think you're going?" he asked. "I thought I told ye to stay out of me sight!"

Gary started shaking and shivering. "Um . . . um . . ." was all he could get out.

"The captain said we could sleep on the beach," Vicky spoke up. She wasn't afraid of Rotten Tooth.

"The cap'n said?" Rotten Tooth laughed.

"AYE!" a voice yelled.

Rotten Tooth stopped laughing when he saw Captain Stinky Beard standing behind him. He looked more frightened than Aaron

did standing over the fish tank. I had to cover my mouth to keep from giggling.

"Sorry, Captain," he said. "But Cap'n? Who will be keeping an eye on these shrimps?"

Captain Stinky Beard made a face. "Surely you've taught them enough by now that they'll be all right until we get back with the treasure."

Rotten Tooth looked at us. "Aye . . . s-surely," he stuttered. "I've taught them plenty," he lied.

But Captain Stinky Beard was already walking away. He called back to Rotten Tooth to get a move on.

"Aye aye!" Rotten Tooth said and hurried off after the rest of the crew, but not before giving us one last rotten look.

We waited until the crew was out of sight. Then I pulled the map out of my pocket.

I looked at the words on the map. *The treasure you seek is not in the feet; head for the head instead.* It was easy to figure out. Since the island was shaped like a snake, it meant the treasure was in the head part.

I looked at the map again. I turned it upside down. Then I turned it backside up. It looked the same both ways.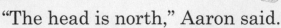

"Which is the head and which is the tail?" Vicky asked.

"The head is north," Aaron said.

"How do you know?" Gary asked.

"Because the head is always at the top, that's how!"

I'd spun the map around so many times, I didn't know which was the top anymore. But then I noticed two lakes that looked like eyes. "That must be the head," I said. Aaron was right. It was north.

Soon the sun began to set behind the *Sea Rat*. We all watched it, waiting for it to get dark. Well, all of us except Inna, who was watching the ground for any signs of snakes.

Vicky looked at the map again. "The crew had a head start. We need a shortcut if we're ever going to get there first."

I took a long look at the map. It said to walk along the beach. That was the way the captain had gone. Vicky was right: We'd never beat them there if we went the same way.

Aaron pointed to the map. He made a straight line from where we were to the treasure. It took us right through the jungle! "That's the way we should go," he said.

It might have been dangerous, but it was the only way.

"We'll leave once the sun sinks into the ocean," I said. Everyone agreed.

"We'll just have to look out for bugs," I warned. "The jungle is full of creepy crawlies."

"BUGS!" Inna shouted. She stuck her tongue out of her mouth and her face turned greenish. "No one said anything about bugs."

Chapter 7
Deep in the Jungle

As soon as it was dark, we headed
out. It was pretty spooky in the jungle.
There were strange sounds all around us.
Everywhere we turned, the glowing eyes
of lizards and bugs followed us. To keep
from being afraid, we talked about how
great it was going to be when we found the
treasure.

"How much treasure do you think
there'll be, Pete?" Gary asked.

"Lots!" I said. I wasn't sure exactly how
much, but "lots" seemed like a pretty good
guess. Captain Stinky Beard wouldn't
go after any treasure that was even one
penny less than lots.

Vicky rubbed her hands together

greedily. "Maybe it'll be enough to buy our own pirate ship!" she said.

"AYE!" Aaron shouted. "We kids could rule it and make Rotten Tooth scrub the dishes!"

I imagined Rotten Tooth, the toughest pirate on the seas, wearing an apron and washing dishes. I had to admit, it was a pretty funny sight. I would've liked to see that.

"Aye, but we can't break the pirate code," I said.

"What pirate code?" Vicky asked.

"The one I learned about on my old ship," I told them.

"Well, what's it say?" Aaron asked.

"It says that a good pirate never betrays the captain," I said. "So no matter how much treasure there is, we're giving it all to Captain Stinky Beard. That's the rule!"

Aaron made a face. "I hate rules."

"Look on the bright side," I told him. "If we give it to the captain, he'll let us come on every pirate adventure! Then Rotten Tooth will *have* to make sure we're ready."

"And we can learn to swashbuckle?"
Aaron asked.

"Aye." I nodded. That seemed to cheer
him up. He picked up a stick from the
muddy ground and began swinging it
around like a sword. He leaped around and
pretended to fight dangerous foes.

Vicky and Gary joined him. The three of
them took off down the path. They swatted
at bugs and leaves and yelled like real
pirates.

Then, all of a sudden, something swatted back!

BOMP!

It swatted Gary right on the forehead. He tumbled backward into a mud puddle.

I rushed toward him with the torch. I came face-to-face with a brown, slimy, dripping mess of a monster!

I almost screamed, but it was only Gary.

"Something hit me," he said, rubbing his forehead.

"What is it? I don't want to look," Inna said, peeking through her fingers, which were covering her eyes.

I shined the torch in front of me. I saw what had struck Gary. It was a huge rock.

"Looks like Gary got attacked by a wall!" Aaron joked.

I looked closer. There was a snake carved on the wall. It pointed to the side. I took a few steps.

"AVAST!" I shouted. "It's not just any rock. It's the entrance to the giant snake's cave . . . and to the treasure."

I jumped up and down.

"Great job, Gary!" I patted him on the back.

"I did a great job?" Gary asked.

"Aye, you found the cave," I told him.

"I did?" he asked. Then he looked up. "I guess I did!" he said with a big smile.

"What do we do now?" Vicky asked.

Inna looked at the map. " 'Follow the cave if you dare; beware the snake's deadly stare!' " she read.

The words made us shiver.

"We either go forward like pirates, or go back like scallywags," I said. Then I took a step forward.

Everyone followed.

"Stick together," I whispered as we all headed into the cave. I couldn't be certain, but I thought I heard a slithering sound echoing in front of us.

Chapter 8
X Marks the Spot

"Arrr! I told you that curse was silly," Aaron said as we made our way deeper into the cave.

So far, we hadn't seen any giant snakes. We did see little snakes. Okay, we saw lots of little snakes. But we saw exactly zero giant ones. And I had to let Inna hold onto the back of my shirt and guide her. She absolutely, positively refused to open her eyes.

"We must be getting close," I said.

The X on the map was only two hundred paces from the start of the cave. That meant it would be double for us, since our paces were kid paces. I tried to keep count, but pirates aren't too good at counting. Most pirates can only count to ten. Still, I knew we had to be close.

I walked faster.

There was no sign of the giant snake. So there was no reason to go slowly and carefully. "Come on, mateys! Let's make sure we beat Rotten Tooth there so we can see the look on his face."

I hurried as fast as I could with Inna tugging my shirt behind me. There was a turn ahead. I had a good feeling about it. I dashed around the corner. "There it is!"

I couldn't even believe my eyes!

I gulped.

In front of me was the biggest, tallest, most giant . . . pile of treasure I'd ever seen in my whole life!

"BLIMEY!" I shouted. I was so happy that I danced around. I didn't even care that pirates aren't supposed to dance.

Aaron ran at the mountain of gold coins and dove in just like he was diving into the ocean. Vicky tossed the coins around like she was splashing in the waves.

Inna still had her eyes covered.

"Look, Inna! We found the treasure.
There's even jewelry," I told her. Inna loved
jewelry!

"Are you sure it's safe to look?" she
asked.

"Sure I'm sure," I told her.

Then Inna took her hands away from
her face and opened her eyes. Her eyes got
real wide and her mouth fell open. I couldn't
blame her; it sure was quite a treasure.

But then it was my turn to bring my hands up to cover something. Only I was covering my ears, because Inna started screaming at the top of her lungs.

Then she pointed.

I turned around.

In front of me was the biggest, tallest, most giant . . . *snake* I'd ever seen in my whole life!

Chapter 9
Aye! Eye-to-Eye!

I poked my head out from behind the rock. I saw the snake slither our way. It looked mean. It looked even meaner than Rotten Tooth covered in stinky fish guts!

Just then, it turned its head toward me. I quickly ducked down.

"That was close," I said. "I almost looked it in the eye."

"What are we going to do?" Gary asked.

There were snakes everywhere. Not just the big one, but little ones, too. "There must be a gazillion of them," Vicky said.

I tried to count them.

"One. Two. Three." Then I lost count. "Aye, a gazillion seems right," I said.

We were trapped!

There was no escape.

"Inna, what did the riddle say again about breaking the curse?" I asked.

Inna spread her fingers apart the tiniest bit. It was just enough so that she could read the riddle. " 'To break the snake's curse, use the curse in reverse.' "

As she read, I caught a glimpse of her necklace. It gave me an idea.

"Inna, can I borrow your necklace?" I asked.

Inna shook her head. "No way!"

"But I need it to defeat the snake," I pleaded.

"Are you going to hypnotize it?" Gary asked.

"Not quite," I said. Then I asked Inna for her necklace again. "Pretty please with sardines on top!" I begged.

"Promise nothing gross will happen to it?"

"I triple promise!" I told her.

Finally, she handed me the necklace. I held it out in front of me and slipped out from behind the rock. I kept my eyes tightly shut.

I could feel the snake slithering right up next to me. Inna's shiny necklace dangled between us.
Then the giant snake leaned in closer. I held my breath.

Suddenly, the hissing stopped.

Everything went quiet.

Then . . . *POOF!*

I took a peek.

The snake was gone! There was an old lady standing there instead.

"WOW!" Aaron said, peeking out from behind the rock.

They all came out from hiding. None of us could believe our eyes!

Then the smaller snakes started to wiggle. Inna screamed and then there were even more POOFs. Each of the little snakes poofed into smoke. And when the smoke cleared, the pirate crew of the *Sea Rat* was standing in front of us.

"Did my necklace do all of *that*?" Inna asked.

"Aye," I said, a little surprised myself. I had broken the curse!

Then we saw that there were other pirates, too. Rival pirates.

"Who are they?" Vicky asked.

"They must have come looking for the treasure before us and were turned into snakes," I said.

The pirates looked at the crew of the *Sea Rat*. We outnumbered them. I counted. There were exactly a lot of us and exactly only a little of them.

"Let's get out of here!" they shouted. They must have counted the same numbers as me.

Captain Stinky Beard rubbed his eyes. "Arrr, how'd you break the curse?" he asked me.

"Just like the clue said. I reversed it," I said. "I saw my reflection in Inna's necklace and figured out the riddle. I just had to make the snake look into its own eyes," I explained.

"Clever lad!" Captain Stinky Beard said. "I thank ye! It's not fitting for a cap'n to be a snake." He was so glad that he didn't even ask how we knew where to look for them.

The old lady was the next one to thank me.

"Aye," I said. "But who are you?"

She told us she'd been cursed a long

time ago. "I was a pirate like you. I tried stealing this treasure from my captain, but he caught me."

I nudged Aaron in the side. "I told you that was against the rules," I whispered.

"Aye," the lady said. "And as punishment, my captain put a powerful curse on me. He turned me into a snake to make sure no one else tried to steal the treasure. I've had to guard that treasure ever since."

"What happened to him?" Vicky asked.

The lady smiled. "He was the first person I turned into a snake," she told us. "I haven't seen him since."

"So whose treasure is it now?" Inna asked.

"Yours!" she said. "I never want to see it again. Take as much as you want."

The whole crew cheered and started filling their pockets.

I felt pretty proud.

And happy, too!

That was, until I felt Rotten Tooth's hand on my shoulder. "ARRR!" he growled. "Who gave you mangy mutts permission to leave the beach? You'll be on kitchen duty for a month!"

We froze in our tracks.

I couldn't believe it. My plan had failed again.

But then Captain Stinky Beard came over. He ordered Rotten Tooth to back off. "This little matey and his friends just saved our lives!" he said. "Not to mention won us this here treasure."

Rotten Tooth was the only one who didn't look so happy about that.

"I won't be having me best pirates washing dishes!" Captain Stinky Beard said. "See to it that they learn everything they want to know. Maybe they might even teach *you* a thing or two," he said.

"HOORAY!" we shouted.

We jumped up and down.

Then the captain winked at us to let us know it was okay to dance around.

We danced the whole way back to the *Sea Rat*! And on the way, we made a list of all the things we wanted Rotten Tooth to teach us. After he took a bath, of course!